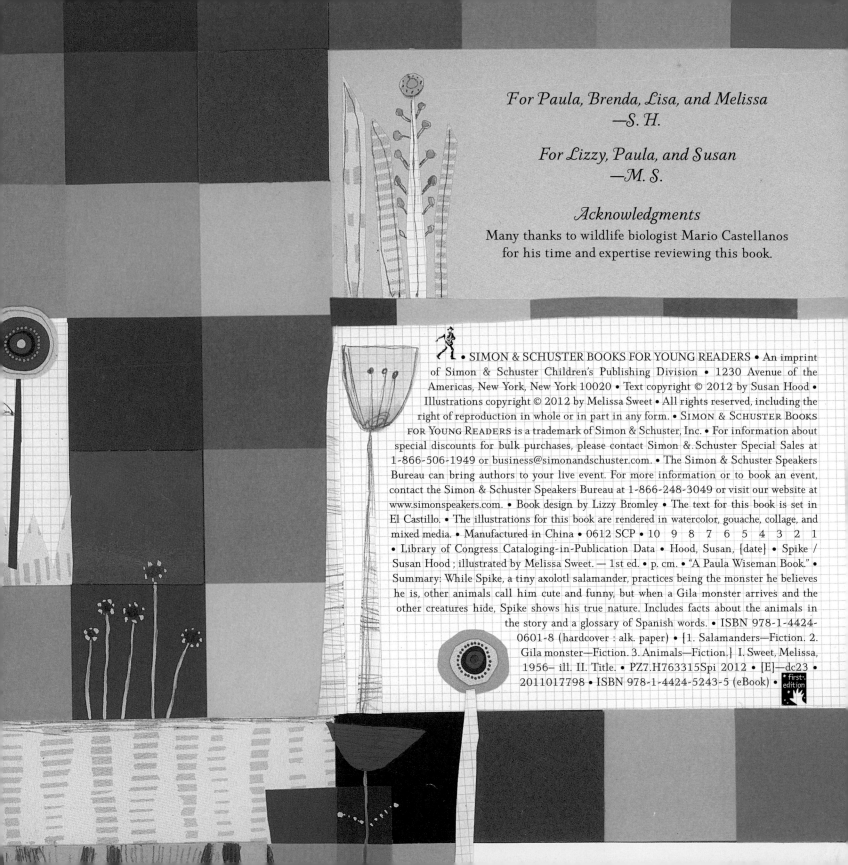

For Paula, Brenda, Lisa, and Melissa
—*S. H.*

For Lizzy, Paula, and Susan
—*M. S.*

Acknowledgments
Many thanks to wildlife biologist Mario Castellanos
for his time and expertise reviewing this book.

• SIMON & SCHUSTER BOOKS FOR YOUNG READERS • An imprint of Simon & Schuster Children's Publishing Division • 1230 Avenue of the Americas, New York, New York 10020 • Text copyright © 2012 by Susan Hood • Illustrations copyright © 2012 by Melissa Sweet • All rights reserved, including the right of reproduction in whole or in part in any form. • SIMON & SCHUSTER BOOKS FOR YOUNG READERS is a trademark of Simon & Schuster, Inc. • For information about special discounts for bulk purchases, please contact Simon & Schuster Special Sales at 1-866-506-1949 or business@simonandschuster.com. • The Simon & Schuster Speakers Bureau can bring authors to your live event. For more information or to book an event, contact the Simon & Schuster Speakers Bureau at 1-866-248-3049 or visit our website at www.simonspeakers.com. • Book design by Lizzy Bromley • The text for this book is set in El Castillo. • The illustrations for this book are rendered in watercolor, gouache, collage, and mixed media. • Manufactured in China • 0612 SCP • 10 9 8 7 6 5 4 3 2 1 • Library of Congress Cataloging-in-Publication Data • Hood, Susan, [date] • Spike / Susan Hood ; illustrated by Melissa Sweet. — 1st ed. • p. cm. • "A Paula Wiseman Book." • Summary: While Spike, a tiny axolotl salamander, practices being the monster he believes he is, other animals call him cute and funny, but when a Gila monster arrives and the other creatures hide, Spike shows his true nature. Includes facts about the animals in the story and a glossary of Spanish words. • ISBN 978-1-4424-0601-8 (hardcover : alk. paper) • [1. Salamanders—Fiction. 2. Gila monster—Fiction. 3. Animals—Fiction.] I. Sweet, Melissa, 1956– ill. II. Title. • PZ7.H763315Spi 2012 • [E]—dc23 • 2011017798 • ISBN 978-1-4424-5243-5 (eBook) •

first edition

Spike,
the Mixed-up Monster

Words by
Susan Hood

Pictures by
Melissa Sweet

A Paula Wiseman Book
Simon & Schuster Books for Young Readers
New York London Toronto Sydney New Delhi

Spike was a monster.
Or so he thought.

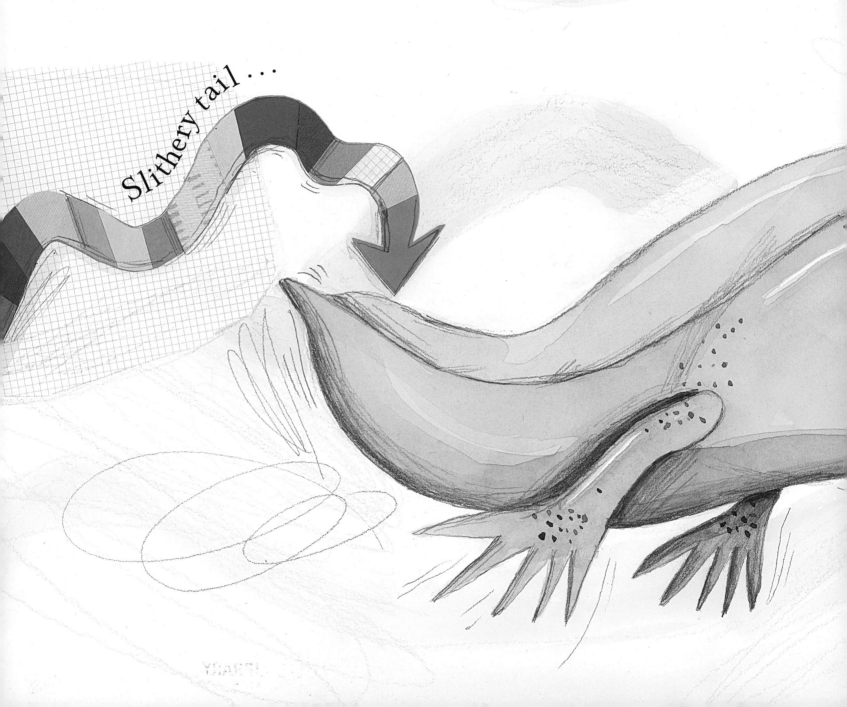

Slithery tail . . .

Spike spent hours practicing his monster moves.

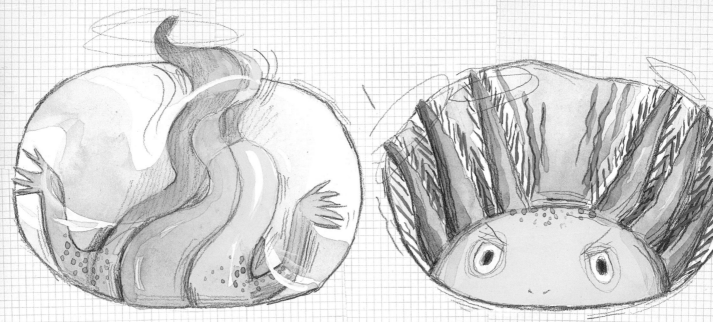

He'd swoosh that tail,   shake those spikes,

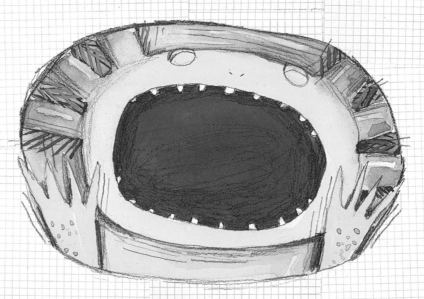

and bare those teeth.

He'd splish, **splash,**
splatter, and
splutter!

There was just one little problem.

Spike was no bigger than a lily pad.
So no one was afraid of Spike.

"Aww, my funny
little fish face,"
quacked *el pato*.

Spike shook
his spikes.

"Ah, *amigo*,"
said *el armadillo*.
"You're cuter than
a bug's behind!"

Spike swooshed
his tail.

"*¡Ay, caramba!*
You're almost as
adorable as I am!"
said *el campañol*.

Spike bared his teeth.

"He has such a sweet smile!"
Everyone agreed.

Spike's crown of spikes drooped and he sank beneath the water, settling into the scum at the bottom of the lake.

I'm a horrible monster,
he thought.
A no-good, horrible monster.

Early one misty morning
a traveler appeared by the lake.

A monster . . .

a real monster . . .

a Gila monster!

He wore a black mask and
flicked a black tongue.

Here was a monster as tough as they come.

One look, and the animals knew what to do.

"*¡El monstruo!*" quacked *el pato.*
"Flap and fly! Flap and fly!"

"¡El monstruo!" cried *el armadillo*.
"Dig and hide! Dig and hide!"

"¡El monstruo!" said *el campañol*.
"Run inside! Run inside!"

Only Spike was left
to face *el monstruo*.

and swooshed his tail.

He splished, splashed, splattered, and spluttered!

El monstruo didn't make a move.

He didn't make a sound.

He stopped and stared.

"Did I scare you?" asked Spike.

"Scare me? No." *El monstruo* laughed.
"It's just that no one has ever smiled
at *me* before."

"Ohhh," said Spike. His crown of spikes drooped as he dropped back down into the water.

"WAIT!" cried *el monstruo*. "Wait, *amigo*, I need your help.
I was headed for my cousin's *fiesta*, but I took a *siesta*. . . .
Now I am lost. Everyone runs away from me, so I have
no one to ask for help."

"Well, *I* can help you," said Spike. And he flashed his fellow monster a big, friendly monster grin as he pointed out the correct path.

"*¡Gracias, amigo!*" said *el monstruo*,
returning Spike's smile.

"*¿Amigo?*" said Spike.
"*De nada, mi amigo.
¡Adiós!*"

"¡Adiós, amigo!"
said el monstruo.
"See you next time!"

And he was on his way.

Slowly, carefully,

el pato,

el armadillo,

and *el campañol*

crept out of their hiding places.

Spike just smiled.

More About Spike and His Amigos

Photo © John P. Clare—Caudata.org

Spike isn't really a monster, but he *is* real. Spike is an **axolotl** (pronounced ACK-suh-LAH-tuhl), a special kind of salamander that can be found in Mexico. Axolotls range in size from 7 to 14 inches long, with the average being between 9 and 10 inches.

Water Monster. The name "axolotl" comes from the native Aztec language (Nahuatl) and means "water monstrosity," "water twin," "water sprite," or "water dog" after the Aztec god Xolotl. Some call the axolotl a Mexican walking fish. The Japanese call it a wooper looper!

Axolotls in the Wild. Axolotls used to be found only in two places in the world—Lake Chalco and Lake Xochimilco (pronounced SO-chee-MEEL-koh) near Mexico City. Today Lake Chalco is gone, drained to avoid flooding. Lake Xochimilco has become a popular tourist spot, where visitors sightsee in gondolas through canals called the Floating Gardens. With the crowds comes pollution. Axolotls are critically endangered, nearly extinct, because of the loss of their natural habitat.

Pets to Get? Many people keep these colorful creatures in aquariums as pets. Axolotls bred in captivity come in a variety of colors—white, pink, yellow, gold, and green.

Mysterious Healing Powers. Axolotls are bred and studied by scientists because of a strange healing power that allows them to completely regrow a lost leg, eye, and even parts of their brain.

Water Babies. Axolotls have a Peter Pan–like ability to avoid growing up. While other salamanders lose their gills and develop lungs that help them breathe on land, not so the axolotls. They live their whole lives and even have children as youthful water babies.

For more information, visit axolotl.org.

Photo © Craig Lorenz/Photo Researchers Inc.

El monstruo is a **Gila** (pronounced HEE-la) **monster**, a 2-foot-long poisonous lizard.

Poison Pals. The Gila monster and its cousin, the Mexican beaded lizard, are the only venomous lizards on earth.

On the Scent. Gila monsters hunt with their tongues. They flick them out to pick up scents in the air.

Legends and Lore. The Gila monster has gotten a bad rap, and not just because of its dangerous bite. Thanks to legend and superstition, the Gila has been falsely accused of spitting venom, leaping high in the air to attack, killing people and animals with its foul breath, and even ridding itself of waste through its mouth!

Shy Guy. In truth, the Gila monster is mostly a slow-moving, solitary animal that lives in dry or desert lands, such as the southwestern United States and northern Mexico. While its bite is painful, it tends to shy away from humans and large animals, spending much of its time underground. Both the Gila and the Mexican beaded lizard face a high risk of extinction in the wild.

El campañol is a **Mexican vole**, which is about the size of a small mouse (4 ½ to 6 inches long), with a short tail and little, rounded ears.

Little Vegetarians. Mexican voles prefer to fill up on grass, leaves, roots, bulbs, berries, nuts, seeds, and bark.

Long in the Tooth. Like all rodents, voles have front teeth that never stop growing. They must keep gnawing to keep their teeth from getting too long.

Traffic Lanes. Voles eat their way through the tall grass, creating well-run lanes, and like to hide under rocks or fallen trees.

Nonstop Nibblers. Voles eat day and night, gobbling their own body weight in twenty-four hours. Imagine if you ate as much as you weigh every day!

Photo © John Mitchell/Photo Researchers Inc.

El pato is a **cinnamon teal duck**, which weighs less than a pound and measures about 16 inches long. It is among the smallest ducks.

Dabbling Ducks. There are two kinds of ducks: dabbling ducks and diving ducks. The cinnamon teal is a dabbling or puddle duck. It favors shallow water and skims the surface of the water for waterweeds, algae, grasses, and seeds.

Bottoms Up! Dabblers can also tip upside down when reaching for food at the bottom of a shallow lake or pond.

Breathing Underwater. The duck's nostrils are set far back from the top of its bill so it can breathe easily while dabbling underwater for food.

Daily Grind. To grind their food, ducks don't use teeth. Instead they swallow small stones and grit that roll around in their gizzards. Once the stones become too smooth to grind, the ducks throw them up and swallow new ones.

Ready for Takeoff. Cinnamon teals are fast flyers. They don't need a running start, but can use their wings to jump straight up from the water. And surprise! What looked like a rusty brown duck in the water suddenly reveals bright blues and greens on its wings in flight!

El armadillo is a **nine-banded armadillo**, which is about the size of a large house cat.

Body Armor. In Spanish, "armadillo" means "little armored one." The top of its body is protected with heavy pieces that are similar to human fingernails when the armadillo is young, but that harden as the animal grows and ages. It has no armor on its underside, only fur and skin.

Bug Hunt. The armadillo usually hunts for food (beetles, flies, ants, earthworms, spiders, slugs, and snails) at night or at twilight, but can also be seen foraging midday.

Disappearing Act. The armadillo is somewhat blind and easily startled. To escape enemies, it can't roll itself into a ball like other armadillos, but can dig a hole so quickly it seems to disappear!

High Jump. If a predator persists, it may be in for a nasty surprise. An armadillo can jump three to four feet in the air, giving its attacker a dislocated jaw!

Cool Tricks. The armadillo can walk underwater, holding its breath for up to six minutes. For wider streams, the armadillo has another nifty trick: It can gulp air to inflate its stomach and intestines and simply float across!

Spanish Words

¡Adiós!: Good-bye!

el armadillo: the armadillo

¡Ay, caramba!: Oh, goodness!

el campañol: the vole

de nada: it was nothing

fiesta: festivities or party

¡Gracias!: Thanks!

mi amigo: my friend

el monstruo: the monster

el pato: the duck

sí: yes

siesta: afternoon nap

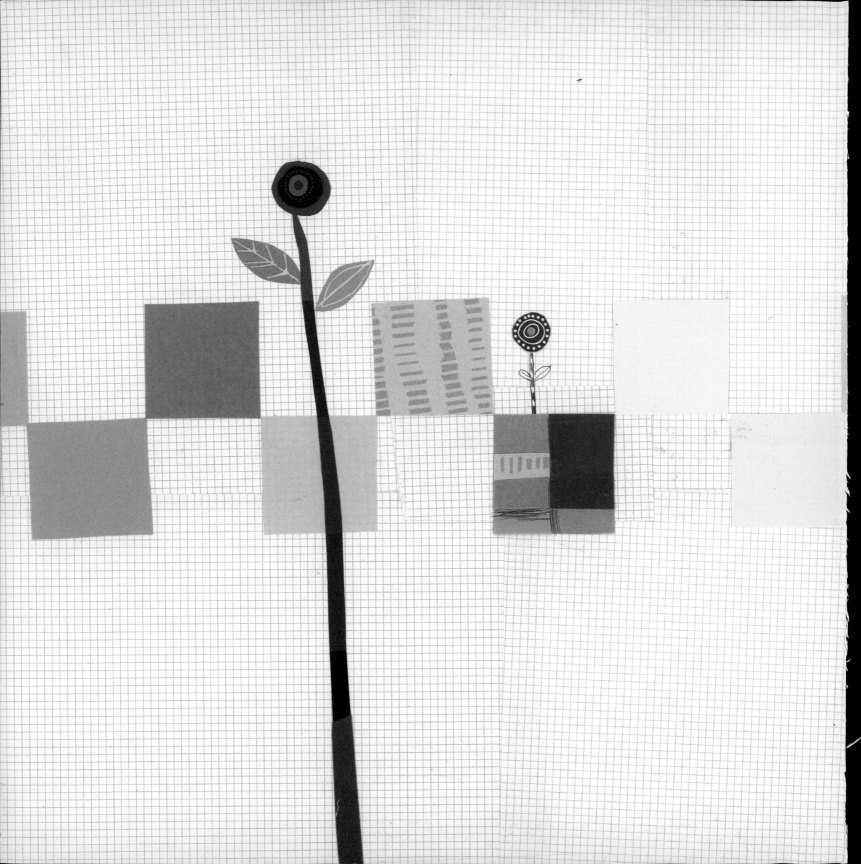